Jazz is color.

Jazz is cool.

HEAVEN'S
ALL-STAR
JAZZ BAND

DON CARTER

ALFRED A. KNOPF ✦ NEW YORK

In memory of jazz
drummer and friend
Joe Cullen.

THIS IS A BORZOI BOOK PUBLISHED BY ALFRED A. KNOPF

Copyright © 2002 by Donald J. Carter
All rights reserved under International and
Pan-American Copyright Conventions. Published
in the United States of America by Alfred A. Knopf,
a division of Random House, Inc., New York, and
simultaneously in Canada by Random House of
Canada Limited, Toronto. Distributed by
Random House, Inc., New York.

www.randomhouse.com/kids

KNOPF, BORZOI BOOKS, and the colophon are registered
trademarks of Random House, Inc.

Library of Congress Cataloging-in-Publication Data
Carter, Don, 1958–
Heaven's all-star jazz band / written and illustrated
by Don Carter.— 1st ed.
p.   cm.
Summary: A young boy imagines his grandfather
playing with jazz music greats up in heaven.
ISBN 0-375-81571-6 (trade)
ISBN 0-375-91571-0 (lib. bdg.)
[1. Jazz—Fiction. 2. Musicians—Fiction.
3. Grandfathers—Fiction. 4. Heaven—Fiction.
5. African Americans—Fiction.] I. Title.
PZ7.C2432 He 2002
[E]—dc21   2001038635

Printed in the United States of America
October 2002
10 9 8 7 6 5 4 3 2 1
First Edition

Grandpa Jack loved jazz.
Salt peanuts. Salt peanuts.

Music by Dizzy, Monk, and Bird,
Lemon meringue pie,
Cadillac cars,
And sardine sandwiches.

Grandpa Jack.
Storyteller extraordinaire,
Jazz aficionado,
Bear hug king.

Jazz was his thing.
Bwaada-bweee-bop
He called it "heavenly."
Bweee-bop-bweee

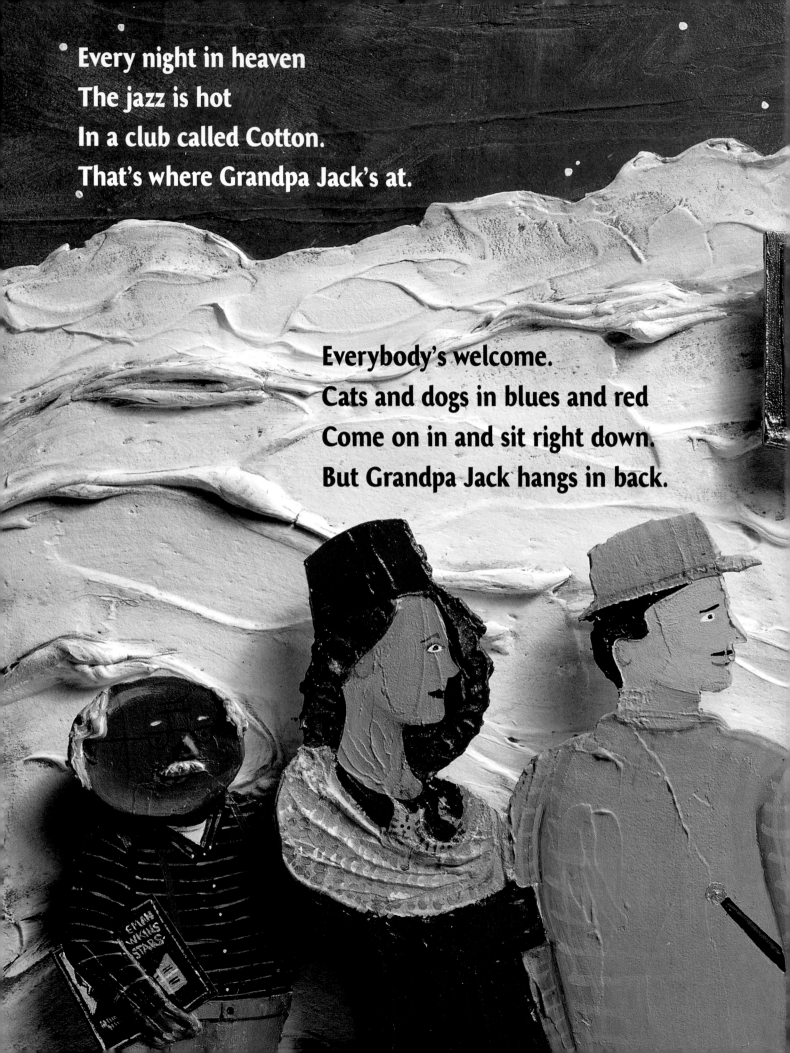

Every night in heaven
The jazz is hot
In a club called Cotton.
That's where Grandpa Jack's at.

Everybody's welcome.
Cats and dogs in blues and red
Come on in and sit right down.
But Grandpa Jack hangs in back.

He's got all their records.
Played 'em loud
When Grandma wasn't looking,
Windows open,
    spaghetti cooking.

Now they're in heaven.
So many famous faces
All on one stage.
Grandpa Jack paces.

STAGE

Mingus plucks his big bass
Soft and low.

Then it gets dark and stormy
When Miles begins to blow.

Grandpa Jack digs jazz.
Salt peanuts. Salt peanuts.

It don't mean a thing
If it ain't got that swing.
That's what Duke says.
And that's what Duke plays.

Grandpa's feet are tappin'.
His fingers are snappin'.
The joint is jumpin'.
The band is really somethin'.

Swing-bop-blues
Monk wears shades
Scat-diddly-dat
And a porkpie hat.

Satchmo is the greatest.
A tisket, a tasket
He sings without words.
Mister scat fantastic.

Jubilation.
Good for Grandpa's circulation.

Grandpa Jack feels jazz.
Salt peanuts. Salt peanuts.

Dizzy's next.
His cheeks are so round
Cubana-be, cubana-bop
Man-oh-man, looks like he's gonna pop.

Grandpa Jack steps closer
To hear Miss Sarah and Ella sing.
But of all the voices heard,
Lady Day he most preferred.

Lady sings the blues.
Grandpa Jack is hypnotized.
Mesmerized.
Rhapsodized.

On wings of gold
Bird solos, Bird soars.
Free at last, Bird.
Free at last.

One-two-three-four.
Basie counts off.
When he strikes up the band,
Everybody lends a hand.

Green suspenders.
Mustard slacks.
Grandpa plays the spoons
While Blakey, on drums, backs.

Grandpa Jack grooves jazz.
Salt peanuts. Salt peanuts.

Jambalaya and black-eyed peas
Hope you like it spicy.
Click-clack-boom-boom
Grandpa Jack gets a little feisty.

Grandpa Jack sings.
Grandpa Jack swings.
Bravo!
Now he has wings.

The crowd roars.
    Trane shakes Grandpa's hand.
        Welcome, sir,
            To Heaven's All-Star Jazz Band.

Now when I hear Satchmo,
Dizzy, Miles, or Bird,
I think of Grandpa Jack
    And smile.

I love you, Grandpa Jack.
Salt peanuts. Salt peanuts.

Heaven's All-Star Jazz Band is:

top row:

MINGUS—Charles Mingus (1922–1979) No band is complete without a bass. The bass plays low-down and deep with a *thump-da-dum-thum-thump*. Sometimes it lays down the beat with the drums. Charles Mingus could lay down the beat with a sound that was both colorful and smooth. But Mingus was also a great composer. He loved to blend different styles in the songs he wrote. Take a listen to his "Goodbye Pork Pie Hat."

MILES—Miles Davis (1926–1991) Miles Davis was cool. He put a lot of emotion into his trumpet playing. But Miles was never satisfied playing one kind of jazz. Over a long career, he played bebop, cool jazz, hard bop, experimental jazz, jazz-rock, and funk. He was a true innovator and left us a long legacy of brilliant music. One of my favorites is his album *Kind of Blue*.

DUKE—Duke Ellington (1899–1974) A thousand songs is a lot of songs to write. But over fifty years, that's at least how many Duke Ellington wrote. While he and his band traveled around the world, Duke was constantly jotting down ideas for songs on any scrap of paper he could find. His "Take the 'A' Train," "Sentimental Lady," and "Mood Indigo" are some of the most famous American songs ever written.

MONK—Thelonious Monk (1917–1982) Thelonious Monk wore such unusual hats, it was hard to predict what he'd wear next. You could say he played his music the same unpredictable way. One minute he'd be playing the piano, and then he'd stop and get up to dance in the middle of the song. His music was filled with pauses so long, some wondered if the song had ended. At first, some people didn't understand Monk's music. But as with abstract art, they grew to appreciate it for its unique beauty. "'Round Midnight" is one song that I appreciate a lot.

middle row:

SATCHMO—Louis Armstrong (1901–1971) Louis Armstrong's trumpet always stood out from the rest of the band. First of all, he played louder than anyone else. And second, he didn't always play the notes he was supposed to. It was called "improvising." He even had his own style of singing, called "scat," which used nonsense syllables instead of words to make his voice sound like a trumpet too. A great sample of scat singing can be heard on his song "Heebie Jeebies."

DIZZY—Dizzy Gillespie (1917–1993) Dizzy Gillespie was so full of energy, he just couldn't sit still. Following in the footsteps of Louis Armstrong, he loved to improvise on the trumpet. He also loved the audience. Sometimes he would wink or wave to someone in the audience behind the bandleader's back. Sometimes his clowning around got him in trouble, but his playing always saved the day. In fact, he has been credited as one of the originators of the bebop style of jazz, which can be heard on his classic "Cubana Be, Cubana Bop."

MISS SARAH—Sarah Vaughan (1924–1990) People called Sarah Vaughan "the Divine One." They also called her "Sassy." And like her nicknames, Sarah's voice had many different personalities. She could sing very high or she could sing very low. She could sound like a scat singer or an opera singer. But whatever way Sarah Vaughan chose to sing, it was breathtaking. "Tenderly" was her first hit song.

ELLA—Ella Fitzgerald (1917–1996) Ella Fitzgerald started singing for the Chick Webb Orchestra after she won a talent contest at the Apollo Theatre. After only a few months, she was very popular with audiences. Over the years, Ella sang many different kinds of music—from bebop to scat to classic and pop—but she always came back to her first love, jazz. One of my favorites is "Mack the Knife." Ella forgot the words and made up her own. It is very funny.

LADY DAY—Billie Holiday (1915–1959) Billie Holiday had a tough life, and when she sang a song she put everything she had into it. Whether it's the sadness in "Stormy Blues" or the bounce of "Them There Eyes," you know exactly how she was feeling at the time. No one else has ever sung like Billie Holiday. And probably no one ever will.

bottom row:

BIRD—Charlie Parker (1920–1955) Charlie Parker played the alto saxophone. But while everyone else was playing big-band music, he helped start a new kind of jazz called bebop. Bebop was like a whole new language. It even sounded like its name—*bee-ba-pa-da-n-bee-bop*. With songs like "Billie's Bounce," "A Night in Tunisia," and "Ko-Ko," Charlie Parker changed the sound of jazz forever.

BASIE—Count Basie (1904–1984) Count Basie and his Orchestra could swing. With a tight rhythm section and the best horn players around, they were the cat's pajamas of the big-band era. Everybody was jumping and jiving to songs like "One O'Clock Jump" and "Jumpin' at the Woodside." Not only did Count Basie make great music, he made great musicians. Many of his band members went on to stardom of their own.

BLAKEY—Art Blakey (1919–1990) Take a look at any picture of Art Blakey playing the drums and what do you see? I see one happy fella. And it showed in his music too. His hard-bop drumming was filled with *rat-a-tat-tat* snare drum rolls and crashing cymbals. Just listen to his band, the Jazz Messengers, play songs like "Moanin'" or "Along Came Betty" and you'll see what I mean.

TRANE—John Coltrane (1926–1967) The music just flowed from John Coltrane's tenor saxophone. It was complicated, passionate, and nonstop. Sometimes it was bursting with energy and sometimes it was soulful and tender. Trane's music had so many layers that it was described as "sheets of sound." You can't listen to just one John Coltrane song. Check out his masterpiece albums *Giant Steps* and *A Love Supreme*.

Jazz is music.

Jazz is rhythm.